SHAKESPEARE

A MIDSUMMER NIGHT'S DREAM

RETOLD BY
NEL YOMTOV

ILLUSTRATED BY
BERENICE MUNIZ

COLORED BY
FARES MAESE

STONE ARCH BOOKS
a capstone imprint

Retold by Nel Yomtov
Illustrated by Berenice Muniz
Colored by Fares Maese

Series Editor: Sean Tulien
Editorial Director: Michael Dahl
Series Designer: Brann Garvey
Art Director: Bob Lentz
Creative Director: Heather Kindseth

Shakespeare Graphics is published by
Stone Arch Books, 1710 Roe Crest Drive,
North Mankato, Minnesota 56003

WWW.CAPSTONEPUB.COM

Cataloging-in-Publication Data is available
at the Library of Congress website.

ISBN: 978-1-4342-2605-1 (library binding)
ISBN: 978-1-4342-3449-0 (paperback)

PRINTED IN THE UNITED STATES OF AMERICA IN
NORTH MANKATO, MINNESOTA.
052015
008920R

TABLE OF CONTENTS

SHAKESPEARE

WILLIAM SHAKESPEARE WAS ONE OF
THE GREATEST WRITERS THE WORLD
HAS EVER KNOWN.

HE WROTE COMEDIES, TRAGEDIES,
HISTORIES, AND ROMANCES ABOUT
ANCIENT HEROES, BLOODY WARS,
AND MAGICAL CREATURES.

THIS IS ONE OF THOSE STORIES . . .

THE COMEDY OF
A MIDSUMMER NIGHT'S DREAM

"The course of true love never did run smooth."

Ancient Greece, in the palace of Theseus, the Duke of Athens . . .

Fair Hippolyta, in four days we shall be married!

Yes, Theseus, and those days shall quickly pass.

I won you with my sword, but I will marry you with joyful celebration.

12

15

Meanwhile, at the home of Quince, several actors meet to rehearse a play that will be performed at Theseus and Hippolyta's wedding.

Our play is a sad comedy called *Pyramus and Thisbe.*

You, Nick Bottom, will play Pyramus, a lover who kills himself.

I will move the audience to storms of tears, Quince!

Flute, you will play the role of Thisbe, the lady that Pyramus loves.

But I have a beard!

Then you shall wear a mask.

ACT
TWO

"I am that merry
wanderer of the night."

"Remember when we saw a mermaid riding a dolphin's back?"

"Flying above, Cupid let loose an arrow from his bow . . ."

Puck, come listen . . .

"Missing its mark, it fell upon a flower."

THUNK!

24

When set on sleeping eyelids, the juice of that flower will make any man or woman fall madly in love with the next creature it sees.

Fetch me that flower, Puck.

When Titania is asleep, I'll drop the juice of the flower on her eyes.

The next thing she looks upon, she shall love!

And before I remove the spell . . .

I'll make her give the boy to me.

32

"And yet, to say the truth, reason and love keep little company together nowadays."

ACT
THREE

43

Nearby, Demetrius wakes up.

Oh, fair Helena – you are a goddess, perfect and divine!

W-what?

Demetrius, must you join Lysander to mock me, too?!

But you love Hermia, Lysander!

All my love for Hermia is gone. I love Helena now!

Look, Lysander – there is your dear.

Lysander, why did you leave me while I slept?

48

ACT FOUR

"I have had a dream, past the wit of man to say what dream it was."

As Titania awakens . . .

Oberon, what strange dreams I have had! I thought I was in love with a donkey!

Oh –! Was it a dream after all?

Come, my queen.

We must leave for Theseus's wedding.

As the sun rises, Theseus and Hippolyta enter the forest, just coming from an early morning hunt.

Why, then we *are* awake — and our dreams have come true!

Let's follow him!

Nearby, Bottom finally wakes up.

I have had a dream, past the wit of man to say what dream it was.

I thought I had become a donkey!

But no one should speak of such a weird dream. I'd be an ass if I even tried to explain it . . .

I will get Quince to write a song about this dream, and I will sing it at the duke's wedding!

ACT FIVE

"If we shadows have offended,
think but this, and all is mended,
that you have but slumber'd here
while these visions did appear."

"Now until the break of day, in this house we fairies stay."

"Hand in hand with fairy grace, we will sing and bless this place . . ."

". . . so all these couples three, shall in true love forever be!"

"Don't delay or stay too long!"

"Meet us at the break of dawn!"

ABOUT THE RETELLING AUTHOR

The career path of **Nel Yomtov** has taken him from the halls of Marvel Comics, as an editor, writer, and colorist, to the world of toy development. He then became editorial and art director at a children's nonfiction book publisher, and now Nel is a writer and editor of books, websites, and comics for children. A harmonica-honking blues enthusiast, Nel lives in New York with his wife, Nancy. They have a son, Jess.

ABOUT THE ILLUSTRATORS

Berenice Muniz is a graphic designer and illustrator from Monterrey, Mexico. In the past, she has done work for publicity agencies, art exhibitions, and she's even created her own webcomic. These days, Berenice is devoted to illustrating comics as part of the Graphikslava crew. In her spare time, "Bere" loves to draw, read manga, watch animated movies, play videogames, and kill zombies.

Fares Maese is a graphic designer and illustrator. He has worked as a colorist for Marvel Comics and as a concept artist for the card and role-playing games Pathfinder and Warhammer. Fares loves spending time playing video games with his Graphikslava comrades, and he's an awesome drum player.

ABOUT WILLIAM SHAKESPEARE

William Shakespeare's true date of birth is unknown, but it is celebrated on April 23rd, 1564. He was born in Stratford-upon-Avon, England. He was the third of eight children to his parents, John and Mary.

At age 18, William married a woman named Anne Hathaway on November 27th, 1582. He and Anne had three children together, including twins. After that point, Shakespeare's history is somewhat of a mystery. Not much is known about that period of his life, until 1592 when his plays first graced theater stages in London, England.

From 1594 onward, Shakespeare performed his plays with a stage company called the Lord Chamberlain's Men (later known as the King's Men). They soon became the top playing company in all of London, earning the favor of Queen Elizabeth and King James I along the way.

He retired in 1613, and died at age 52 on April 23rd, 1616. He was buried at Holy Trinity Church in Stratford. The epitaph on his grave curses any person who disturbs it. Translated to modern English, part of it reads:

> *Blessed be the man that spares these stones,*
> *And cursed be he who moves my bones.*

Over a period of 25 years, Shakespeare wrote more than 40 works, including poems, plays, and prose. His plays have been performed all over the world and translated to every major language.

THE HISTORY
BEHIND THE PLAY

Shakespeare was inspired by many other works when he wrote *A Midsummer Night's Dream*. For example, the story of *Pyramus and Thisbe*, from Ovid's *Metamorphoses*, played an important role in the creation of Shakespeare's play. It served as a basis for several parts of the play's plot, and is even included in *A Midsummer Night's Dream* as a play-within-a-play! *Pyramus and Thisbe* was also an inspiration for *Romeo and Juliet*, another of Shakespeare's most popular play.

Greek mythology served as a basis for several of the character's names in *A Midsummer Night's Dream*. In Ancient Greek myths, Lysander was a mythological Greek warlord, Theseus was the King of Athens, and Hippolyta was the Queen of the Amazons — a race of fierce, female warriors.

While *A Midsummer Night's Dream* had many inspirations, it has also influenced modern culture. For example, when William Herschel, a British astronomer, discovered the two moons circling the planet Uranus in 1787, he named them Oberon and Titania in honor of the king and queen of the fairies.

No one knows for certain when *A Midsummer Night's Dream* was first written or performed. Nevertheless, the play has been performed across the globe for hundreds of years. It has also been recreated as musicals, operas, ballets, books, movies — and graphic novels like this one.

SHAKESPEAREAN LANGUAGE

Shakespeare's writing is powerful and memorable — and sometimes difficult to understand. Many lines in his plays can be read in different ways or can have multiple meanings. Also, the English language was not standardized in Shakespeare's time, so the way he spelled words was not always the same as we spell them nowadays. However, Shakespeare still influences the way we write and speak today. Below are some of his more famous phrases that have become part of our language.

FAMOUS LINES FROM A MIDSUMMER NIGHT'S DREAM

"The course of true love never did run smooth." (Act I, Scene I)

SPEAKER: Lysander

MODERN INTERPRETATION: **True love always faces obstacles.**

EXPLANATION: Lysander explains to Hermia that being in love is always difficult because so many things have to be considered when two lovers want to be married.

"I am that merry wanderer of the night." (Act II, Scene I)

SPEAKER: Puck (Robin Goodfellow)

MODERN INTERPRETATION: **That's me, I am the playful Robin Goodfellow, also known as Puck.**

EXPLANATION: Puck, a playful fairy-sprite, plays tricks on others on Oberon's behalf. Puck identifies himself formally as Robin Goodfellow, but most fairies know him simply as Puck.

"And yet, to say the truth, reason and love keep little company together nowadays." (Act III, Scene I)

SPEAKER: Bottom

MODERN INTERPRETATION: **To tell you the truth, logic and love rarely go hand in hand these days.**

EXPLANATION: Titania, under a spell of love, falls in love with Bottom at first sight. Bottom, not knowing he has the head of a donkey, remarks that she has no reason to love him. He then adds that, lately, love hasn't been making much sense at all.

"I have had a dream, past the wit of man to say what dream it was." (Act IV, Scene I)

SPEAKER: Bottom

MODERN INTERPRETATION: **I was dreaming! My dream was so strange that I couldn't even explain it if I tried.**

EXPLANATION: Bottom wakes up without his donkey head, and thinks that the entire experience of falling in love with Titania was only a dream.

"If we shadows have offended, think but this, and all is mended, that you have but slumber'd here while these visions did appear." (Act V, Scene I)

SPEAKER: Puck

MODERN INTERPRETATION: **If you, the viewer, did not like anything that happened in this play, then relax — it was all just your dream.**

EXPLANATION: Puck breaks the "fourth wall" and speaks directly to the audience of the play. He tells them that they should not worry if they were offended, or they did not like what they saw during the play, because they only dreamt the whole thing.

1. Of all the characters in *A Midsummer Night's Dream*, which one was your favorite? Why?

2. This play is considered to be a comedy. Did you think it was funny? Why or why not?

3. Do think Theseus was a fair ruler in this book? What about King Oberon? What makes for a good ruler?

WRITING PROMPTS

1. Magic and spells are used to distract, confuse, and control characters in this book. Think up a magic spell of your own. What does it do? How do you cast it? Write about your spell. Then draw a picture of your spell in action.

2. In the play, Oberon and Titania fight over an Indian boy. In Shakepseare's time, fairies were said to steal children and keep them as servants. Imagine that you are kidnapped by fairies for a day. Write about your experiences as the son or daughter of a fairy king and queen.

3. The performance of *Pyramus and Thisbe* in *A Midsummer Night's Dream* is called a play-within-a-play. Write your own one-page play, including several characters, a story, and dialogue.

"ALL THE WORLD'S A STAGE."

— WILLIAM SHAKESPEARE